Grandy's Recipe for Tear Soup

Helpful ingredients to consider

- a pot full of tears
- one heart willing to be broken open
- a dash of bitters
- a bunch of good friends
- many handfuls of comfort food
- a lot of patience
- buckets of water to replace the tears

- plenty of exercise
- a variety of helpful reading material
- enough self care
- season with memories
- optional: one good therapist and/or support group

Directions:

Choose the size pot that fits your loss. It's okay to increase pot size if you miscalculated. Combine ingredients. Set the temperature for a moderate heat. Cooking times will vary depending on the ingredients needed. Strong flavors will mellow over time. Stir often. Cook no longer than you need to.

Suggestions:

- be creative.
- trust your instincts.
- cry when you want to, laugh when you can.
- freeze some soup to use as a starter for next time.
- keep your own soup making journal so you won't forget.

Serves: one

To Bill Weeks, my first hospice patient 25 years ago, and his wife Nancy.
To Chuck and Dana, who taught me to not be afraid. To the bereaved parents
in the Compassionate Friends, Parents of Murdered Children, Brief Encounters,
and Suicide Bereavement Support groups, and the members of the AIDS support
groups, who have been my patient teachers.
- P.S.

To my best friend Annie for believing in me.
To our children Morgan & Connor. And to my parents,
for encouraging me with their passion for life.
- C.D.

To Lisa and Madison, for all their love and patience,
and for letting me stay up late to whittle away at page after page...
And to Ray & Jean Bills for their continued support
of their rather unconventional kids.
- T.B.

Tear Soup

A RECIPE FOR HEALING AFTER LOSS

Story by

Pat Schwiebert and Chuck DeKlyen

Illustrated by

Taylor Bills

Grief Watch Portland, Oregon USA

There once was an old and somewhat wise woman whom everyone called Grandy.

She just suffered a big loss in her life. Pops, her husband, suffered the same loss, but in his own way. This is the story of how Grandy faced her loss by setting out to make tear soup.

For many years the custom of making tear soup had been forgotten. As peoples' lives became more rushed they found it much easier to pull "soup in a can" from the shelf and heat it on the stove.

But several years ago Grandy got a taste of a well-seasoned tear soup. One of her friends made it from scratch after her child died.

As soon as Grandy tasted the rich flavor of that carefully made soup, she promised herself never again to assume that quicker was better.

Because of her great loss Grandy knew this time her recipe for tear soup would call for a big pot.

With a big pot she would have plenty of room for all the memories, all the misgivings, all the feelings and all the tears she needed to stew in the pot over time.

She put on her apron because she knew it would get messy.

It seems that grief is never clean. People feel misunderstood, feelings get hurt and wrong assumptions are made all over the place.

To make matters worse, grief always takes longer to cook than anyone wants it to.

6

And then...

Grandy started to cry.

At first she sobbed.

Sometimes she wept quietly.

And sometimes when she was in a safe place where no one could hear her...

she even wailed.

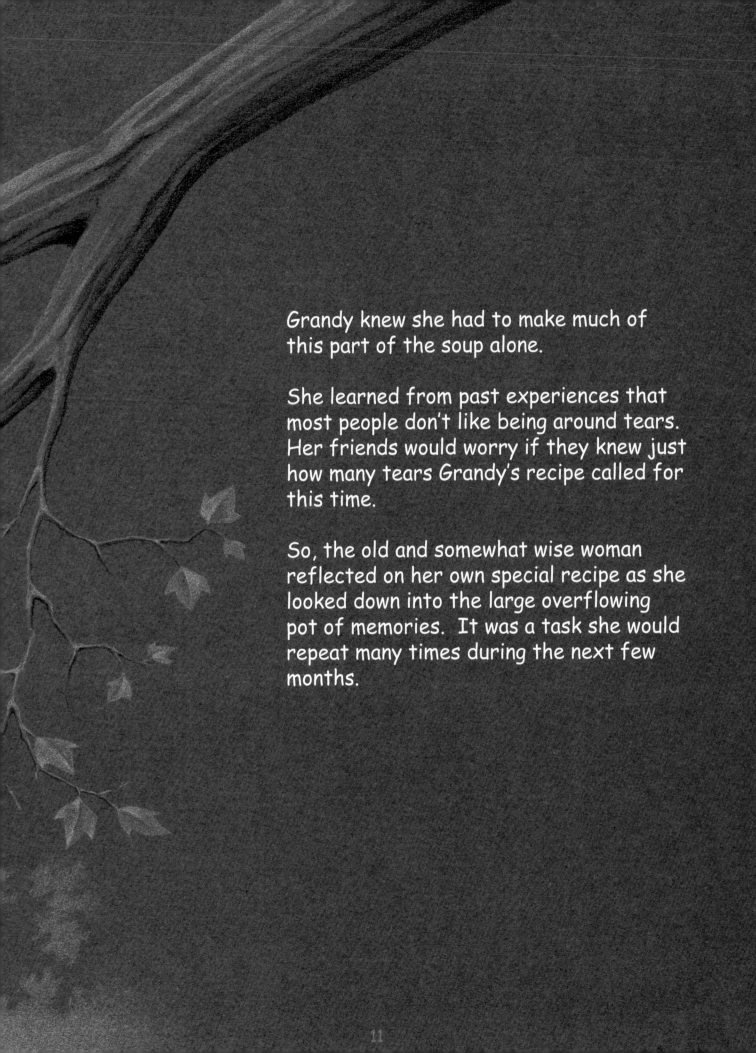

Grandy knew she had to make much of this part of the soup alone.

She learned from past experiences that most people don't like being around tears. Her friends would worry if they knew just how many tears Grandy's recipe called for this time.

So, the old and somewhat wise woman reflected on her own special recipe as she looked down into the large overflowing pot of memories. It was a task she would repeat many times during the next few months.

Grandy winced when she took a sip of the broth.

All she could taste was salt from her teardrops.
It tasted bitter, but she knew this was where
she had to start.

And for now, it was the only thing on *her* menu.

There were things that Grandy never wanted to forget.

These included the good times and the bad times, the silly and the sad times.

With her arms
full of memories
Grandy made
many trips to the
kitchen.

One at a time,
she slowly
stirred all her
precious and not
so precious
memories into
the pot.

But eventually she ran out of things to add.

Grandy's arms ached and she felt
stone cold and empty.

There were no words that could
describe the pain she was feeling.

What's more, when she looked out
the window it surprised her to see
how the rest of the world was
going on as usual while her world
had stopped.

Her grandson, Chester, who just wanted his Grandy to be happy again, hoped his chocolate drops would make her feel better.

Mrs. Bloomklotz, Ms. Chadwick and Mr. Long, all brave yet fearful neighbors, dropped by to see how Grandy was doing.

They filled the air with words, but none of their words took the smell of tear soup away.

Grandy was gracious because she knew how helpless her friends felt. They wanted to fix her, but they couldn't. All Grandy really needed from them at that moment was a knowing look and a warm hug.

There were also days when Grandy hungered for a
thoughtful ear.

Sometimes she would ask total strangers,
"Care to join me in a bowl of tear soup?"

"No thanks," most would reply, "I don't have time for
tear soup today."

Even some of Grandy's friends hurried past her
house and pretended not to notice the aroma of tear
soup coming through her open door.

Grandy found that most people can tolerate only a
cup of someone else's tear soup. The giant bowl,
where Grandy could repeatedly share her sadness in
great detail, was left for a few willing friends.

"I'm here," Midge cried. "I got here as fast as I could and I'll be here whenever you need me. What a tragedy. I'm so sorry you're having to make such a big pot of soup."

 Oh what a relief. Grandy knew she didn't have to be careful what she said around Midge.

Midge wouldn't try to talk her out of anything she was feeling. And Grandy could even laugh and not worry that Midge would assume Grandy was over her grief.

"Sorry I couldn't get here sooner," said Midge.

"No problem," replied Grandy. "I've had plenty of help. But most of these friends will be history pretty soon. They'll be over my tragedy long before I am. But I know you'll still be around."

"I don't know what to say, but I'll be glad to listen," Midge said tenderly. "C'mon, tell me all about it while we make some bread to go along with your soup."

These two friends, who had shared a thousand laughs and just as many tears, pounded at the bread dough together.

"I feel like I'm unraveling." Grandy cried. "I'm mad. I'm confused. I can't make any decisions. Nobody can make me feel good. I'm a mess. I just didn't realize it would be this hard."

"Why don't we go for a walk while we wait for the bread to rise," Midge suggested.

"I know exercise is supposed to help me but I feel like I have concrete blocks strapped to my legs. We'd better not go too far or you'll have to carry me home," moaned Grandy.

Mrs. Cries-a-lot called and reminded Grandy that she had been making tear soup for years and would be more than glad to come right over and show her how to make it the correct way.

"Thanks but no," said Grandy. "This pot has my name on it."

Grandy knew better than to let Mrs. Cries-a-lot or anyone else tell her what she should do to get through this terrible loss.

Next her recipe called for some comfort food.

For Grandy this meant mashed potatoes or ice cream. Comfort food always makes you feel better--at least for a little while. It gets past that big lump in your throat when other foods can't.

"I think it needs some chocolate too." After all, it was her soup.

Grandy kept attending worship even though she was mad at God.

Sometimes she yelled at God and asked why this happened. And sometimes she demanded to know where God was when she was feeling so all alone.

Still, Grandy trusted God, but she didn't understand God.

She sensed that people believed that if she really had faith she would be spared deep sorrow, anger and loneliness. Grandy kept reminding herself to be grateful for ALL the emotions that God had given her.

On some afternoons people would ask questions like,

"Is it soup yet?" Or,
"How long is it going to take? You have been at this
for over a month now. It's time to get out of the kitchen."

Grandy fumed at the caller's advice.

Grandy looked forward to getting the mail each day. She dreaded the day when no more sympathy cards would come.

When she was alone and needed to think she found it helpful to keep notes on her soup making.

FROM THE KITCHEN OF GRANDY

10/6 Today I'm upset that I have to be making this soup.

FROM THE KITCHEN OF GRANDY

11/21 I don't think anyone remembers that I'm making soup from scratch.
11/29 What's the use, life seems to be so hard

FROM THE KITCHEN OF GRANDY

3/28 I'm beginning to like the taste of this soup. I think I could live on it forever.

3/29:

M THE KITCHEN OF GRANDY

a book, shoveled lk, and talked dont want to anymore, but it's temporary.

Thank goodness Grandy and Pops have been married a long time.
They already knew each other's tear soup would be different.

Secretly Grandy wished Pops would put more flavoring in his
soup, but he doesn't want to. And he's perfectly content to dine
alone and sip his own soup.

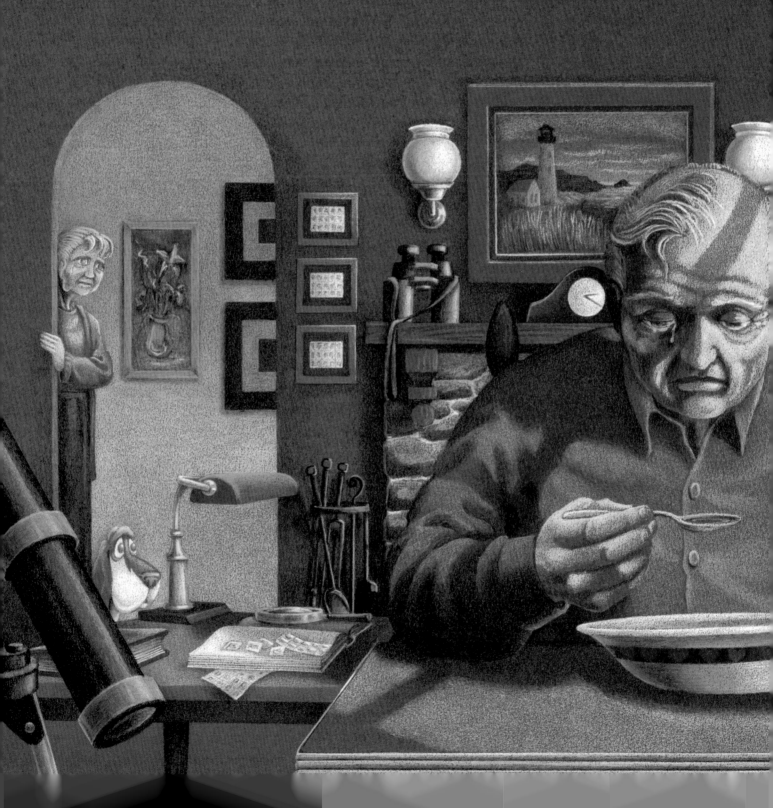

Making tear soup is hard work.

Sometimes it was all she could think about. Even the things Grandy used to love to do, she didn't have the energy for, nor did she care about anymore.

Some of Grandy's friends over the years had not tended to their tear soup. Their soup boiled over and the pot scorched.

What a mess. It took them a long time to clean up their pots and to start over. The smell of burnt soup still lingers in some of their homes.

Grandy knew there were times when she needed to take a break from her soup making. Even though it was hard to do, she forced herself to get away.

Grandy heard that a neighbor was having to take her turn in the kitchen. Some people thought that the neighbor was eating too much tear soup.

So Grandy, being an old and somewhat wise woman, called and invited her to a special soup gathering where it's not bad manners to cry in your soup or have second helpings.

Soon the thoughtful cooks sat at Grandy's table and discussed the process of making tear soup. There are some parts that require help from friends and some parts you just have to do alone. They shared stories about soup making they wouldn't dare tell anyone else for fear of being judged a bad cook.

They all laughed knowingly when Grandy remarked, how on days when she was daydreaming while driving, she was glad that the car seemed to know where she wanted to go.

These people had become Grandy's "new best friends."

One day as Grandy and Chester were going for a drive, Chester asked, "Mom says you've been making tear soup. What does she mean?"

"Well, tear soup is a way for you to sort through all the different types of feelings and memories you have when you lose someone or something special. Remember when your baby brother died right before he was born and your mom sat for days holding his blanket and weeping? She was making tear soup."

"You made tear soup yourself by acting out your own disappointment when you shouted at Jason, wishing his brother would die, too."

"Remember when Billy's dog died and he didn't want to play with you? Not feeling like having fun is one of the ingredients of tear soup, also."

"And remember when Aunt Meg got divorced and they had to move? There was a lot of tear soup simmering in that house."

"Some days when you're making tear soup it's even hard to breathe. Some days you feel like running away. You just hope a better day comes along soon. And then comes one of the hardest parts of making tear soup,"

"It's when you decide it may be okay to eat something instead of soup all the time."

The next morning as Grandy was cleaning up, Chester asked her if she was done making tear soup.

"Well, I don't think you actually ever finish. The hard work of making this batch of soup is almost done though. I'll put the rest in the freezer and will pull it out from time to time to have a little taste."

"So what else have you learned by making tear soup, Grandy?"

"I've learned that grief, like a pot of soup, changes the longer it simmers and the more things you put into it. I've learned that sometimes people say unkind things, but they really don't mean to hurt you."

"And most importantly, I've learned that there is something down deep within all of us ready to help us survive the things we think we can't survive."

"Grandy, you know so much.   What will I do after you die?"

"Don't worry, I will leave you my recipe for tear soup."

Grandy's Cooking Tips

- Grief is the process you go through as you adjust to the loss of anything or anyone important in your life.

- The loss of a job, a move, divorce, death of someone you love, or a change in health status are just a few of the situations that can cause grief.

- Grief is both physically and emotionally exhausting. It is also irrational and unpredictable and can shake your very foundation.

- The amount of "work" your grief requires will depend on your life experiences, the type of loss, and whatever else you have on your plate at that time.

- A sudden, unexpected loss is usually more traumatic, more disruptive and requires more time to adjust to.

- If your loss occurred through violence, expect that all the normal grief reactions will be exaggerated.

- You may lose trust in your own ability to make decisions and/or to trust others.

- Assumptions about fairness, life order, and religious beliefs are often challenged.

- Smells can bring back memories of a loss and a fresh wave of grief.

- Seasons, with their colors and climate, can also take you back to that moment in time when your world stood still.

- You may sense you have no control in your life.

- Being at work may provide a relief from your grief, but as soon as you get in the car and start driving home you may find your grief come flooding back.

- You may find that you are incapable of functioning in the work environment for a short while.

- Because grief is distracting it also means you are more accident-prone.

- The object of grieving is not to get over the loss or recover from the loss but to get through the loss.

- Over the years you will look back and discover that this grief keeps teaching you new things about life. Your understanding of life will just keep going deeper.

If you are the cook

- This is your grief—no one else's. Your friends can't feel your loss in the same way. It will not affect their life the way it affects yours. And you may resent them for that.

- At first you may think dying would be preferable to having to go through this pain. Just try to stay alive. Sudden mood swings are normal. You may suddenly be unreasonable and short.

- Try your best to educate your friends about what you need and how they can help. Be as honest as you can be about how you are feeling.

- Don't give up on your friends if they let you down. But if they continue to be insensitive to your grief you may need to distance yourself for a while until you get stronger.

- At first you will probably want to talk to as many people as possible, but after a month or so, find one or two people whom you can count on for the long haul to just be there and listen when you need to talk.

- Write your thoughts in a journal. It will help you to process and also to remember the new insights you are learning.

- Consider attending a support group. Go at least three times before deciding if it is helpful to you.

- Be open to counseling.

- Exercise, sleep, drink plenty of fluids, and eat a well balanced diet.

- Pamper yourself. Take bubble baths. Get a massage.

- Try not to compare your grief with another's. You don't earn points for having a more painful experience than someone else has. And you won't feel less grief if someone else's loss is worse.

- You deserve to feel happy again. Being happy doesn't mean you forget. Learn to be grateful for the good days.

- Don't be too hard on yourself.

- Long after everyone else has forgotten your loss, you will continue to remember. Learn to be content with your private memories.

If your friend is the one
who is making Tear Soup

- Be there for your friend, even when you don't understand.

- Be a source of comfort by listening, laughing, and crying.

- Stick close to your friend and defend their right to grieve.

- Allow your friend to make mistakes… or at least to grieve differently from the way you would grieve.

- Send flowers. Send money if you know this would help.

- Send cards. The message doesn't need to be long. Just let them know you haven't forgotten them. Send one every few weeks for a while.

- Call your friend. Don't worry about being a bother. Let your friend tell you if they don't want to talk about their loss right now.

- Answering machines and e-mail are great ways to keep in touch allowing the bereaved person to respond only when they feel up to it.

- Try to anticipate what your friend may need. Bereaved persons sometimes don't know what to ask for.

- Avoid offering easy answers and platitudes. This only invalidates grief. Be patient. Don't try to rush your friend through their grief.

- Give your friend permission to grieve in front of you. Don't change the subject or tell them not to cry or act uncomfortable when they do cry.

- Ask them questions. But don't tell them how they should feel.

- Invite your friend to attend events together, as you normally would. Let them decide if they don't want to attend.

- Don't assume because your friend is having a good day that it means they are over their loss.

- Be mindful of holidays, birthdays and anniversaries.

Soup Making and Time

- Grief work takes time. Much longer than anyone wants it to.

- If a child or spouse dies it may be a year before the bereaved begins to gain a sense of stability, because the loss is highlighted by each season, holiday, anniversary or special day. The second year is not so great either.

- You may be okay one minute but the next minute you may hit bottom.

- Nighttime can be particularly difficult. Some people have trouble getting to sleep while others have trouble staying asleep. And then there are those who don't want to wake up.

- Most people can tolerate another's loss for about a month before wanting the bereaved person to get back to normal.

If a child is the cook

- Be honest with the child and give simple, clear explanations consistent with the child's level of understanding. Be careful not to overload them with too many facts. This information may need to be repeated many times.

- Prepare the child for what they can expect in a new situation such as, going to a memorial service, or viewing the body. Explain as best you can how others may be reacting and how you would like the child to behave.

- When considering if a child should attend a memorial service consult the child. Their wishes should be the main factor for the decision. Include the child in gatherings at whatever level they want to participate. Helping to make cookies for the reception may be all they want to do.

- Expect them to ask questions like, "Why does he have his glasses on if he's dead and can't read?" Or, "Why is her skin cold?"

- Younger children are more affected by disruptions in their environment than by the loss itself.

- Avoid confusing explanations of death, such as, "gone away", or "gone to sleep." It might be better to say, "his body stopped working."

- Avoid making God responsible for the death. Instead say, " God didn't take your sister, but God welcomed her." Or, "God is sad that we're sad. But now that your sister has died, she is with God."

- Don't assume that if the child isn't talking about the loss it hasn't affected them.

- Be consistent and maintain the usual routines as much as possible.

- Encourage the child to express their feelings and to ask questions.

- Children may act out their grief in their fantasy play and artwork.

- If children have seen adults cry in the past they will be less concerned about tears now.

- Show affection and let them know that they are loved and will be taken care of.

- Each child reacts differently to loss. Behaviors that you may observe include: withdrawal, acting out, disturbances in sleeping and eating, poor concentration, being overly clingy, regression to earlier stages of development, taking on attributes of the deceased.

- Sharing your grief with a child is a way to help them learn about grief.

If you are a male chef

- The world may not see you the bereaved person that you are. Because of your gender, in our society you may be seen only as the support person--a role you probably play very well.

- If you have been taught from an early age that "big boys don't cry," you may feel ashamed of your own tears. Other people may also be uncomfortable with your tears.

- Don't hold your grief in. Find a safe place or someone who is not afraid of your grief.

- People may tell you how strong you are when you hold in your grief. Don't confuse grieving with weakness and not grieving with strength. In fact, holding grief in is very hard on your body and can weaken your health.

- Gender does not *determine* your grieving style, but it may *affect* the way you grieve.

- Assume that your initial response to grief is the right response for you at that time. Try not to behave as others think you should--but as you need to.

If there are two of you cooking

- Grief is unique to the individual. You may both experience the same loss, but you won't grieve in the same way. In other words, you are in it together, but you are in it alone.

- At first you may feel closer to each other than ever before. But that may change the farther you get away from your shared loss.

- Try not to judge each other.

- Talk to each other when you can.

- Don't let your partner be your only source of comfort.

- Write each other notes.

- It is normal to want others to grieve the same way you grieve and to communicate the same way you communicate. But life is just not that easy.

- Sexual desire may be affected. You both need intimacy, but not necessarily sex. Talk about it.

- Remember the past, hope for the future, but live in the present.

Where to find help

We now have available, 24 hours a day, online support groups and other resources to help in our grieving times. Because there are thousands of websites relating to loss and grief issues we've only listed some of the larger ones. At these locations you will find links to many other good sites.

Grief Watch /Perinatal Loss (that's us) 2116 N.E. 18th Ave. Portland, OR 97212 (503) 284-7426 Resources for pregnancy loss & support for general loss. Site includes a relative links index, message boards, and related grief topics. Also includes information regarding The Remembering Heart, The Certificate of Life, personal bereavement cards, and more. www.griefwatch.com

National Share Office 300 First Capitol Dr. St Charles, MO 63301 (800) 821-6819. This is a national group offering support for parents who have experienced a pregnancy loss, including a national directory of support groups. www.nationalshareoffice.com

The Compassionate Friends (TCF) National Chapter P.O. Box 3696 Oak Brook, IL 60522-3696 (877) 969-0010. This is a national support group for bereaved parents, siblings and grandparents who have experienced the death of a child at any age. www.compassionatefriends.org

Parents of Murdered Children (POMC) National Headquarters 100 Eighth Street #B41 Cincinnati, OH 45202 (513)721-5683. This is a national support group for parents and other co-victims of homicide. www.pomc.com

Centering Corporation 7230 Maple Street, Omaha, NE 68134 (402) 553-1200. Centering has some of the best resources for persons experiencing any type of loss. www.centering.org

The Dougy Center is the National Center for Grieving Children and Families and an internationally known model for providing peer support groups for grieving children, teens, and families. www.dougy.org

Kids Said is a safe place for kids to share and help each other deal with grief about any of their losses. At this site they can share feelings, show their art work, meet with peers online. http://kidsaid.com

Growth House has the "best of the net" resources in most major grief categories, including children's grief. www.growthhouse.org

Web Healing is an interactive website for those healing from loss. Has lots of links to other sites. www.webhealing.com

1000 Deaths is an excellent resource for those who have experienced the death of a loved one by suicide. www.1000deaths.com. Because we who are left behind die a thousand deaths trying to understand why.

AARP has a grief and loss page that offers comprehensive source of information designed to help bereaved adults as well as professional providers of bereavement support. Toll free (866) 797-2277 9A-9p ET www.aarp.org/griefandloss

Divorce Care is a special support group offering information and interaction as you recover from the hurt of divorce. (800) 489-7778; P.O. Box 1739, Wake Forest, NC 27588 www.divorcecare.com

Divorce Transitions offers links, resources, support, newsletter for those in the throes of divorce. www.divorcetransitions.com

A Place to Remember has support materials and resources for those who have been touched by a crisis in pregnancy or the death of a baby. www.aplacetoremember.com

Association for Pet Loss and Bereavement is a site full of support through links, chat rooms and resources for grieving pet owners. www.aplb.org

The Mental Health Net Directory can help you find a therapist in your area. Site also has over 9000 resources relating to mental health issues. www.mentalhelp.net

American Association of Suicidology has excellent links to suicide related topics. www.suicidology.org

There are hundreds of **Recovery Resource** links at www.soberrecovery.com

Resolve. The National Infertility Association contains information, physician referral, message boards. (888) 623-0744; 1310 Broadway, Somerville, MA 02144 www.resolve.org

International Council of Infertility Information Dissemination (INCIID) contains fact sheets, journal summaries, directory of professionals, chat rooms for a variety of related topics. www. inciid.org

Those wanting more information and insight about **Near Death Experiences** of children should visit *Into the Light.* Contains scientific research, newsletter, message board. www.melvinmorse.com/light.htm

Victims of violence will want to go to the Victim-Assistance online. Though it is designed for professionals, it has a wealth of information that would be helpful to anyone wanting to understand the impact violence has on the individual. www.vaonline.org

GriefNet is an internet community of persons dealing with grief, death and major loss. They have 37 email support groups and two web sites. www.griefnet.org

Tear Soup is now available on video!

Running Time: Approx 17 min.
ISBN: 0-9724241-0-5

The same poignant story and engaging illustrations that have made *Tear Soup* a treasured book for people of all ages are given new life in this video version. Viewers will find themselves returning again and again to this moving portrayal as part of their ongoing process of healing from grief. Families, professionals, educators and support groups will all benefit from the insights and comfort provided in this helpful production.

- **Narrated by Mary McDonald-Lewis**

- **Viewers guide & grief tips included**

- **Recommended for all age groups**

Especially helpful for...

Families
Classroom Settings
Churches
Support Groups

For more information please visit www.griefwatch.com

Grief Watch

2116 NE 18th Avenue

Portland, Oregon 97212

(503) 284-7426

(503) 282-8985 fax

email: info@tearsoup.com

web page:: www.tearsoup.com

Text Copyright © 1999 Grief Watch

Illustrations Copyright © 1999 Taylor Bills

Library of Congress Card Catalog Number 97-92835
ISBN 0-9615197-6-2

This is a third edition copy of Tear Soup: April, 2003

The original illustrations were created with
Berol Prismacolor pencils on Canson colored paper.
Color separations and pre-press by Negative Perfection.
Printed by Dynagraphics Portland, Oregon.
Bound by Lincoln & Allen Portland, Oregon.

Conceptualized, conceived and birthed in the warmth of the
18th Ave. Peace House, Portland, Oregon

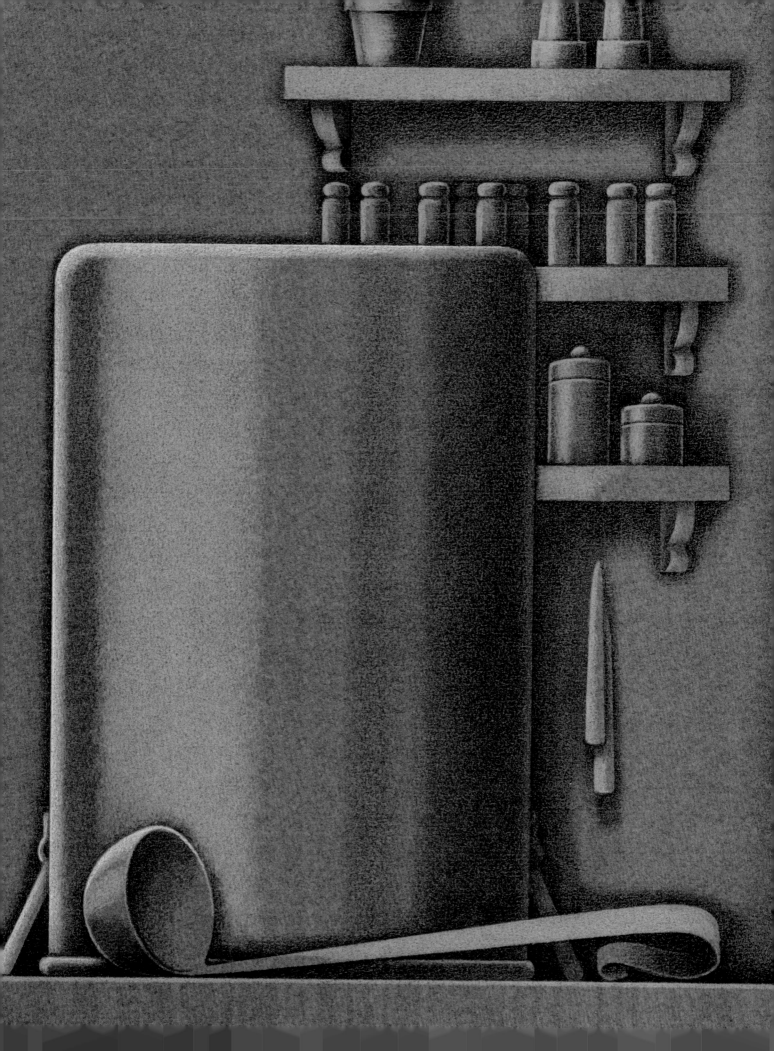